Fast Facts About Bugs & Spiders

Fast Facts About
DRAGONFLIES

by Julia Garstecki

PEBBLE
a capstone imprint

Pebble Emerge is published by Pebble, an imprint of Capstone.
1710 Roe Crest Drive, North Mankato, Minnesota 56003
www.capstonepub.com

Library of Congress Cataloging-in-Publication Data
Names: Garstecki, Julia, author.
Title: Fast facts about dragonfiles / by Julia Garstecki.
Description: North Mankato, MN : Pebble, an imprint of Capstone, [2021] | Series: Fast facts about bugs & spiders | Includes bibliographical references and index. | Audience: Ages 6–8 | Audience: Grades 2–3 | Summary: "Zip! Something darts through the air. It's a dragonfly! Young readers will get the fast facts on these speedy insects, including their body parts, habitats, and life cycles. Along the way, they also will uncover surprising and fascinating facts! Simple text, close-up photos, and a fun activity make this a perfect introduction to the dazzling world of dragonflies." —Provided by publisher.
Identifiers: LCCN 2020031930 (print) | LCCN 2020031931 (ebook) | ISBN 9781977131515 (hardcover) | ISBN 9781977132680 (paperback) | ISBN 9781977154194 (pdf) | ISBN 9781977155900 (kindle edition)
Subjects: LCSH: Dragonflies—Juvenile literature.
Classification: LCC QL520 .G37 2021 (print) | LCC QL520 (ebook) | DDC 595.7/33—dc23
LC record available at https://lccn.loc.gov/2020031930
LC ebook record available at https://lccn.loc.gov/2020031931

Image Credits
Dreamstime: Evgeniya Murashova, 21; Newscom: imageBROKER/Dirk Funhoff, 17, Photoshot/NHPA/Stephen Dalton, 15; Shutterstock: Aliaksei Hintau, cover, Anan Suphap, 13, Andi111, 18, biker11, 6, Ger Bosma Photos, 9, Lane V. Erickson, 5, Martin Pelanek, 4, Mega Pixel, 20 (top right), Pheobus, 19, riphoto3, 20 (bottom right), SeDmi, 20 (top left), Shevs, 8, SweetLemons, 20 (middle right), timquo, 20 (bottom left), trgrowth, 11, Wayne Wolfersberger, 7, zabavina (background), cover and throughout

Editorial Credits
Editor: Abby Huff; Designer: Hilary Wacholz; Media Researcher: Jo Miller; Production Specialist: Tori Abraham

Printed and bound in the USA. PO 3837

Table of Contents

Words in **bold** are in the glossary.

All About Dragonflies

Whiz! A dragonfly zigs and zags in the air. It's an **insect**. It has a long body. It has long wings. Dragonflies come in many colors. There are more than 2,500 kinds.

You can find dragonflies near ponds, lakes, and streams. They live around the world. But they don't live where it is very cold all year long.

A dragonfly's body has three sections. On its head are two short **antennae**. It also has two large eyes. The eyes see in almost every direction.

antenna

eye

wings

legs

The middle part of a dragonfly has six legs. It has four wings. The last body part is long and thin. It can curl up and down.

Zoom! Dragonflies are fast. They fly faster than any other insect. They can flap all four wings at once. This helps them speed through the air.

Dragonflies can also move each wing on its own. This lets them fly backward. They can also move to the sides. They can even fly in place.

A Dragonfly's Life

A female dragonfly lays eggs in the water. A **nymph** hatches from each egg. The nymph is a dull color. It has no wings. It lives in the water. It eats and grows.

Finally, the nymph has grown enough. It climbs out of the water. It sheds, or **molts**, its skin. Now it is a dragonfly!

Dragonfly Life Cycle

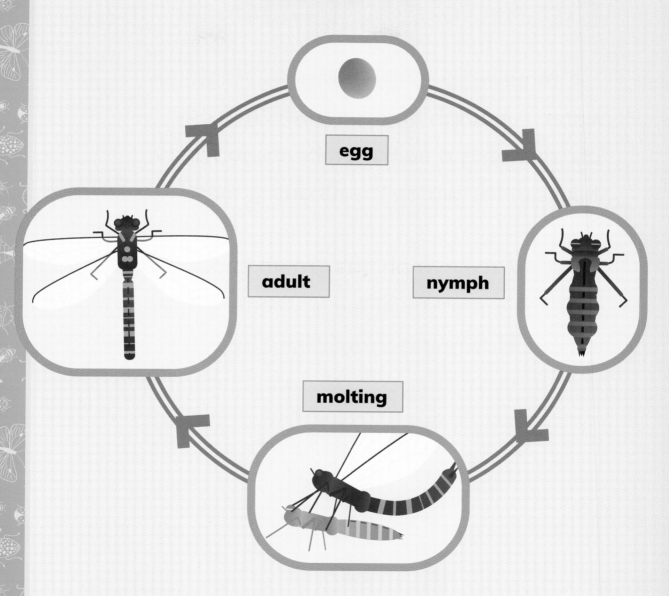

egg

nymph

molting

adult

Catching a Meal

Dragonflies are great **predators**. Some wait on plants. They watch for bugs. They chase any that fly by. Other dragonflies hunt in the air. They fly all day.

A dragonfly uses its legs to catch **prey**. Its legs make a shape like a basket. They scoop up bugs. Dragonflies eat flying insects. That includes mosquitoes, bees, and flies.

13

Nymphs are good hunters too. They hunt in the water. They feed on small insects and tiny fish. How? A nymph has a special bottom lip. The lip shoots out. It has spikes on the end. These catch prey. The nymph pulls back its lip. It eats its meal.

A dragonfly nymph catches a fish.

Swarms

Dragonflies live alone most of the time. But sometimes many come together. This large group is called a **swarm**. A swarm may have millions of dragonflies.

Swarms happen when a lot of prey is in one spot. The dragonflies hunt together. Swarms also happen in a fire or storm. Bugs fly away. Dragonflies chase them.

Fun Facts

- A dragonfly can reach speeds of up to 38 miles (61 kilometers) per hour.

- Dragonflies need to be warm in order to fly. Some sit in the sun. Others shake their wings to warm up.

- The first dragonflies lived more than 300 million years ago. Their wingspan was more than 2 feet (0.6 meters) long!

- Chomp! Dragonflies can eat their own weight in 30 minutes. They even eat other dragonflies.

Make a Dragonfly

What You Need:

- craft stick
- yarn or markers
- two pipe cleaners
- glue
- two googly eyes

What You Do:

1. Decorate the craft stick by wrapping it in yarn or coloring it with markers.

2. Bend both ends of one pipe cleaner to the middle. It should look like an eight. Repeat with the other pipe cleaner.

3. Glue the pipe cleaners to the craft stick to make wings. Glue the googly eyes to the other side of the stick.

Glossary

antenna (an-TEH-nuh)—a feeler on an insect's head used to touch and smell

insect (IN-sekt)—a small animal with a hard outer shell, six legs, three body sections, and two antennae

molt (MOLT)—to shed an outer layer of skin; after molting, a new covering grows

nymph (NIMF)—a young form of an insect; nymphs grow into adults by molting many times

predator (PRED-uh-tur)—an animal that hunts other animals for food

prey (PRAY)—an animal hunted by another animal for food

swarm (SWORM)—a large group of insects gathered or flying together

Read More

Bestor, Sheri Mabry. *Soar High, Dragonfly!* Ann Arbor, MI: Sleeping Bear Press, 2019.

Davidson, Lauren. *The Backyard Bug Book for Kids.* Emeryville, CA: Rockridge Press, 2019.

Peterson, Megan Cooley. *Dashing Dragonflies: A 4D Book.* North Mankato, MN: Pebble, 2019.

Internet Sites

Dragonflies and Damselflies
dkfindout.com/us/animals-and-nature/insects/dragonflies-and-damselflies

Dragonflies—Most Charming Among All Flying Insects
easyscienceforkids.com/all-about-dragonflies/

Dragonfly Facts
coolkidfacts.com/dragonfly-facts-for-kids/

Index